The Berenstain Bears

GET STAGE FRIGHT

Playbill

Most little bears like to play,
To show off, read aloud, and to sing.
But on a stage in the spotlight,
For some — the play's not the thing.

A FIRST TIME BOOK®

FRIGHT

Random House 🏠 New York

Copyright © 1986 by Berenstains, Inc. All rights reserved under International and Pan-American Copyright Conventions. Published in the United States by Random House, Inc., New York, and simultaneously in Canada by Random House of Canada Limited, Toronto.

Library of Congress Cataloging-in-Publication Data: Berenstain, Stan. The Berenstain bears get stage fright. SUMMARY: Sister Bear worries about her lines in the school play while Brother Bear has no fear. Guess who forgets the lines during the performance? [1. Bears—Fiction. 2. Plays—Fiction] I. Berenstain, Jan. II. Title. PZ7.B4483Beof 1986 [E] 85-25716 ISBN: 0-394-87337-8 (trade); 0-394-97337-2 (lib. bdg.)

Manufactured in the United States of America

18   19   20

On the way to school one day Sister Bear, Brother Bear, and Cousin Freddie got to talking about an important subject: their teachers.

"Teacher Bob is tough but fair," said Freddie, who was in the same class as Brother.

Brother agreed. "How about your teacher?" he asked Sister. "Is she easy or hard?"

"Teacher Jane isn't easy *or* hard," Sister said. "She's *good*."

Then the bell rang and the cubs were ready for the school day.

The reason Sister thought Teacher Jane was good was that she made things interesting. When they were learning to add and subtract, Teacher Jane set up a pretend store with play money and a toy cash register. It helped the cubs learn, and it was fun.

When the class was studying words and ideas, they made posters. That helped them learn too.

And sometimes in reading class, instead of just reading from their books, they acted out the stories.

That's what they were doing with *Grizzlystiltskin*, the story of the funny old elf-bear who was sure that nobody could ever guess his name. Sister Bear was acting out the part of the miller's daughter who becomes a princess and has to spin straw into gold. They had come to the part where the princess has one last chance to guess the elf-bear's name:

"'Ah, good sir,'" read Sister in a loud, clear voice.

"'We've come to the end of our guessing game, because I say...*Grizzlystiltskin* is your name!'"

That's when Grizzlystiltskin flies into a rage and disappears in a puff of smoke—and the princess lives happily ever after.

"That was very good, class," said Teacher Jane. "So good, in fact, that I have a surprise for you. I'm in charge of the school play this year, and guess what—the play is going to be *Grizzlystiltskin*, and some of you will have parts in it!"

Then she gave out the parts. One of them had Sister's name on it. What fun! What excitement! Sister was going to be in the school play on the auditorium stage with scenery and costumes and makeup and everything!

It turned out that Brother and Freddie had gotten parts too. Brother was going to be the woodsbear who finds out the elf-bear's name, and Freddie was going to play the part of Grizzlystiltskin himself.

"Who are you going to be?" Freddie asked Sister.

When Sister, who hadn't even thought to look, turned to her part, it said THE PRINCESS.

"Wow!" said Brother and Freddie. "That's the main part!"

"Well, how about that!" said Papa Bear when he heard the news. "My little princess is going to play the part of the princess! Say, we'd better tell Grizzly Gramps and Gran! And Uncle Willie and Aunt Min!"

"Calm yourself, dear!" said Mama, taking Papa aside. "Sister has a lot of work ahead of her and she doesn't need a lot of fuss and excitement."

"Hmm," said Papa. "You're absolutely right, my dear."

"Yeah, why all the fuss?" said
Brother. "It's just a dopey school
play. I already know my whole part...

"'Hear me, oh, Princess!
I was deep in the forest
and this is what I heard:
The princess's firstborn
shall be mine!
If she had guesses
nine times nine,
she could not win
this guessing game,
'cause *Grizzlystiltskin*
is my name!'

"See?" he said.
"Nothing to it!"

But Sister wasn't so sure.
She was beginning to feel
a little nervous about the
whole thing.

The next day, when Teacher Jane asked Sister to take a message to the office, Sister decided to take a shortcut through the auditorium. She had been in the auditorium many times, of course, but she had never been on the stage. She climbed the steps and looked out over the rows of seats. It looked enormous.

Then she imagined all the seats
filled with everybody in the school
and Grizzly Gramps and Gran and Uncle
Willie and Aunt Min. It looked even
more enormous.

"Why the long face?" asked Brother on the way home from school. Sister told him she was worried about the play.

"Relax," he said. "There's nothing to it. It's a piece of cake.

"Why, I can do my part standing on my head...

HEAR ME, OH, PRINCESS...

"...hanging from a branch...

and from inside a hollow log!"

Cousin Freddie and the gang thought Brother was pretty funny. But Sister didn't even smile.

That evening Sister's worries all came out.

"Reading a part in class just isn't the same as getting up in front of the whole school! And I have to learn it all by heart!" she wailed. "How am I ever going to do it?"

"The same way you learn anything else," said Mama. "Line by line, page by page. Papa and I will help you.

"Besides, you already know lots of things by heart—the alphabet, dozens of songs and rhymes, the Pledge of Allegiance. Why, I bet you know enough things by heart to fill a book.

"You already know the story. All you have to do is learn your part and practice."

That's what Sister did. She learned her part line by line, page by page.

And she practiced.

She practiced in her room in front of her toys.

OH, GOOD SIR....

She practiced in the field in front of her forest friends.

WE'VE COME TO THE END OF OUR GUESSING GAME....

She practiced in front
of Mama and Papa.

BECAUSE GRIZZLYSTILTSKIN IS YOUR NAME!...

"That was wonderful, Sweetie!"
said Papa, applauding.
"Letter perfect!"

"Yes," sighed Sister, "but practicing in front
of my toys and forest friends and you and Mama
just isn't the same as getting up on the stage
in front of the whole school. How do I
practice for that?"

"Sweetie," said Mama, "there are some things
in life you can't practice—you've just got
to *do* them."

"But what if I get nervous and scared?" she asked.

"Oh, but you *will*," said Mama.

"I will?" she said.

"Of course!" said Mama. "Everybody gets nervous when they have to perform in front of an audience— even famous opera singers and star athletes. But if you know it's natural and you expect to be a little nervous, it won't really bother you that much—and you'll do yourself proud!

"And besides," she added, "you'll be having a big rehearsal in the auditorium. That'll help. Now, where's that brother of yours? I've got to finish his costume. I do wish he'd take this thing a little more seriously."

"Don't worry about him, Mama," said Sister. "He can do his part standing on his head."

The rehearsal did help, but an empty auditorium still wasn't the same as a real live audience.

And now, at last, the moment had come!
The curtain was opening on the Bear
Country School's production of
Grizzlystiltskin!

And there was Sister all alone on the big stage looking out at the whole school *and* Grizzly Gramps and Gran and Uncle Willie and Aunt Min. It *was* a little scary. But it was also very exciting. Then she heard a loud, clear voice saying, "I am the miller's daughter and woe is me, for my father has told the king I can spin straw into gold and, in truth, I cannot!"

It took her a split second to realize that the voice was *hers*!

From there on everything went beautifully.
There was one little rough spot near the
end when it was time for Brother to do his
part. He came on stage in his handsome
woodsbear costume, looked out at the
hundreds of eyes staring at him...
*and completely forgot what he was supposed
to say!*

"I can't remember my lines!" he
whispered.
"Why don't you try standing on
your head?" whispered Sister. But
then she took pity on him and helped
him with his lines.

The play ended magnificently
with Grizzlystiltskin flying into
a fury and disappearing in
a puff of smoke.

The applause was long
and loud.

After the show Mama and Papa came backstage.
"Terrific show!" said Papa. "Terrific!"
"Congratulations," said Mama, "on a job well done!"
"A piece of cake," said Princess Sister.